DEDICATION

For Blake

THANKS

To my awesome husband—I couldn't do this without you.

To my parents who have always loved my stories and drawings.

To my friend Jessica Grondahl for the push to represent the boys!

Sometimes I have a yucky tummy,

and it just won't let me eat.

But I need food to make me strong,

so I can jump and swing!

I have lots of body parts,

from my head down to my toes.

And I have something extra,

that really helps me grow!

Sometimes I might use my mouth,

to eat up all my food.

But even when I can't,

I have my special tube.

We squirt or bolus the food right in

using a special syringe,

Or we can use a feeding pump

to slowly drip it in.

For the days I'm on the go,

I wear a special pack.

It holds my food and feeding pump

and I carry it on my back!

If my tubey ever hurts,

we can rub on a special cream.

And every night at bath time,

I make sure my stoma is clean!

When I go to bed at night,

sometimes I use my tube.

We turn on the pump

and hang up my bag of food.

With my tubey I have energy

to jump and play with joy,

So I can be a healthy,

and happy little boy!

MY TUBEY GLOSSARY

Bolus: A method of tube feeding that delivers a large amount of food over a short period of time, similar to typical eating patterns. It allows freedom of movement so the child isn't tethered to a feeding bag for long periods, but may not be tolerated by all children.

Cream: Referring to barrier creams that may help with an irritated stoma area, such as Calmoseptin, Triamcinolone Acetonide Cream, or OTC cortisone creams.

Feeding Pump: A programmable electronic pump that can disperse formula or blenderized foods at a rate and volume of your choosing during tube feeds.

Gravity Feed: A method of tube feeding whereby a large syringe vessel is filled with formula, attached via extension set to the feeding tube, and suspended above the child to flow freely with no help from a pump. A caregiver can adjust the height of the syringe to adjust the rate of flow.

G-Tube: Refers to a Gastrostomy. This is a surgically placed feeding tube placed directly into the stomach. Others include those that go into the nose, through the esophagus, and down to the stomach (Naso-Gastric/NG-Tube), and the Jejunum (J-Tube or GJ-Tube), which is the beginning of the intestines. There is also TPN, or Total Parenteral Nutrition, which bypasses the digestive system and delivers nutrients intravenously.

Pack: Refers to a small backpack that can hold a feeding pump, a bag of formula, and an ice-pack. It is worn on the back while the child is being tube fed and gives the child greater mobility.

Stoma: An opening from inside to outside the body. G-Tubes and J-Tubes create a stoma via their channel into the body.

Syringe: Tube feeders have syringes that are specially designed to fit together with feeding tubes and their extension sets so you can administer medications, formula, blenderized foods, and water either by gravity feed, or by pushing it in.

OTHER TUBE FEEDING TERMS

<u>AMT Mini-ONE Button</u>: A type of low-profile G-Tube. Sits closer to the body so is less noticeable and great for active children.

<u>Blenderized Diet</u>: An alternative to canned enteral formulas, using real foods that you prepare yourself at home, blend with a high powered blender, and deliver via feeding tube.

<u>Extension Set</u>: Tubing that you attach during tube feeding, between your G-Tube and your syringe or feeding pump. These sets allow complete range of motion by rotating within the feeding port during movement.

<u>Granulation Tissue</u>: Pink or red, bumpy tissue around the tube/stoma. Bleeds easily and may create mucous.

<u>Mic-Key Button</u>: A type of low-profile G-Tube. Sits closer to the body so is less noticeable and great for active children.

<u>PEG Tube</u>: Often the first G-Tube that is placed, and is replaced several months later with a low-profile G-Tube. PEG stands for Percutaneous Endoscopic Gastrostomy.

CONDITIONS THAT MAY REQUIRE A FEEDING TUBE IN CHILDREN

Aspiration
Brain Injury
Cancer
Celiac Disease
Chromosome Disorders
Cystic Fibrosis
Eosinophilic Disorders
Food Allergies
GERD (Gastroesophogeal Reflux Disease)
Heart Conditions
Mitochondrial Disease
Motility Disorders
Prematurity
Rare Diseases
Respiratory Conditions
Structural Abnormalities
Unknown Diseases/disorders

MORE BOOKS FROM THE MY TUBEY SERIES

My Tubey: A Day in the Life of a Tube Fed Girl (Available Now)
978-1460923085, $12.99 paperback (www.MyTubeyBooks.com to order)

There's More Than One Way to Eat! (Coming June 2011)
Featuring colorful illustrations showing children with every kind of feeding tube—NG, G, GJ, J, TPN and also eating by mouth. Great for educators with a tube fed child in class!

Bye-Bye Tubey: It's Time to Remove My Tube! (Coming August 2011)
If your child has a date set for removing his or her feeding tube, it can be a scary prospect. After all, their tube has become a part of their body and now it's going to be removed! Help ease anxiety and fear with this informative, colorful book that shows a child going to the doctor with mom to get her tubey taken out.

My Tubey Goes to Preschool (Coming September 2011)
Follow along as a tube fed child goes to preschool and plays with new friends! Full-color illustrations address the challenges of being tube fed at school.

HELPFUL RESOURCES

- www.MyTubeyBooks.com
- www.MyTubey.org
- www.babycenter.com (support forum: search for "Babies and Children with a Feeding Tube")
- www.blenderizeddiet.com
- www.BundieBaby.com
- www.cdhnf.org (Children's Digestive Health and Nutrition Foundation)
- www.FeedingEssentials.com
- www.feedingtubeawareness.com
- www.iffgd.org (International Foundation for Functional Gastrointestinal Disorders)
- www.infantrefluxdisease.com
- www.naspghan.org (North American Society for Pediatric Gastroenterology, Hepatology and Nutrition)
- www.Oley.org
- www.PAGER.org
- www.YouStartWithATube.com
- www.tubefedkids.ning.com (forum/support group)

Printed in Great Britain
by Amazon.co.uk, Ltd.,
Marston Gate.